CAMP ROCK

SECOND
SESSION
#4

Hidden Tracks

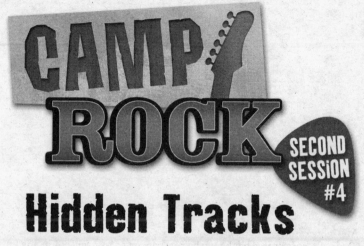

Hidden Tracks

By Helen Perelman

ased on "Camp Rock," Written by Karin Gist & Regina Hicks and Julie Brown & Paul Brown

DISNEP PRESS

New York

Library of Congress Catalog Card Number on file.
ISBN 978-1-4231-1774-2

For more Disney Press fun, visit www.disneybooks.com
Visit DisneyChannel.com

CHAPTER ONE

"I need chocolate!" Mitchie Torres sang out as she walked into Camp Rock's canteen. The B-Note was where campers and counselors could go to get treats. It was also a great place to hang out after the evening program. Located in the basement of the Mess Hall of Fame, the room was filled with old couches, tables, a vintage jukebox, and an old Ping-Pong table. There were usually a bunch of campers jamming in the corner stage area, and tonight was no exception. It looked like just about the entire camp was there.

"Make that a frozen chocolate bar," Caitlyn Gellar said, waving a hand in front of her face. Camp Rock was in the middle of a serious heat wave. Temperatures had been over ninety-five degrees for the last two days, and there had been no clouds in sight. Even though it was evening, the air was still warm and sticky. Caitlyn swept her light brown hair up off her neck and into a loose ponytail.

"Definitely frozen!" Mitchie said, blowing her long bangs up off her forehead. "That sounds like just what I need."

Caitlyn smiled. Even though Mitchie was a relative Camp Rock newbie, she knew all about the perks of a frozen canteen treat.

As the two friends walked over to the snack-bar window to place their orders, Caitlyn noticed Brown Cesario. "Hey, check out Brown," she said. "He's totally jamming over there!" She pointed to the back corner of the room where their camp director was playing guitar.

Barron and Sander, two of the most talented guys at camp, were singing along with him. It was a reggae song that had a catchy melody. Peggy Dupree and Colby Miller were singing backup. Caitlyn's smile grew wider. She loved being at a place where there was an opportunity for creating music every moment of the day. It was *the* place to learn how to be a rock star.

However, there was only one *official* rock star at camp. That was Shane Gray, the lead singer of the hot band Connect Three. Shane had met the two other members of the band at Camp Rock. They had had a pretty quick rise to fame. As a result, Shane had gotten a bit spoiled.

When he started getting bad press for his antics on a video set, his label "suggested" that he come up to camp for the summer to unwind. Brown was his uncle, so he had an easy in. While it had *not* been Shane's idea of a good time, the break had served him well. Not only were Connect Three's sales soaring, he was having a pretty good summer hanging out with the campers—especially Mitchie.

Frozen chocolate bars in hand, Mitchie and Caitlyn headed over to the old couch in the corner of the lounge. There were a few lava lamps scattered around, giving the place a soft glow. The windows were open to let in the hot summer breeze. Mitchie sighed as she settled onto the worn couch.

Even though she felt as if she were melting, Mitchie wouldn't have wanted to be anywhere else at that moment. Thanks to her mom scoring a job as the Camp Rock cook, she'd been able to spend her whole summer there. It was a dream come true and more—the experience had surpassed all her expectations.

Just then, Shane appeared at the canteen

entrance and caught Mitchie's eye.

"Hey, there," Shane called as he crossed the room. He swung his guitar case off his shoulder and plopped down next to her on the couch, eyeing her frozen chocolate bar. "That looks pretty good," he said. "I might need one of those, too."

Before Mitchie could respond, another voiced perked up. "Do you want me to get you one?" Tess Tyler asked, rushing over to Shane. Tess was the resident camp diva. She was usually surrounded by her entourage of Ella Pador and Lorraine Burgess and was constantly looking for a way to get close to Shane and his fame.

"Lorraine," Tess barked to the redheaded girl behind her. "Why don't you go get Shane one of those."

Lorraine was a relatively new member of Tess's entourage. She had arrived for the second session of camp and, when she moved into Vibe Cabin, had quickly fallen in as one of Tess's adoring fans. Mitchie liked Lorraine. She was sweet and a supertalented costume designer. Mitchie had to respect her for that, even if she questioned her taste in friends.

Mitchie wasn't one to judge, though. When she first came to Camp Rock, she had told a huge lie about her mother being a famous music executive just to impress Tess. But Mitchie had quickly learned that lying was not the best way to make friends at camp. When everyone found out the truth, Mitchie got to see who her real friends at camp were—and Tess was not one of them!

But Caitlyn was. Now she and Mitchie exchanged smirks at Tess's latest attempt to cozy up to Shane.

"I'll get it. Thanks anyway," Shane told Tess, standing up. He went up to the snack-bar window. A few minutes later, he returned with his own frozen treat and sat down next to Mitchie once again.

"How was your meeting with Dee?" Mitchie asked when he was settled. She had seen Shane and a few other full-time counselors sitting with Dee La Duke, Camp Rock's musical director, after dinner. It looked as if they were plotting something big.

"Long." Shane sighed. "And we *still* didn't finish! I never knew how much planning goes into each Camp Rock activity. And I'm just a guest instructor!"

"Well we thank you for all your hard work," Caitlyn said, grinning.

Shane smiled and looked over at Brown. "So, listen, after my uncle finishes, I was going to try playing a new tune for you guys," he said nonchalantly.

"Great!' Mitchie exclaimed. She loved listening to Shane sing. If he had a new song, she definitely wanted to hear it.

Shane's dark eyebrows arched. "I think you'll like it, but you'll have to be totally honest with me."

"You got it," Mitchie agreed, nodding. Caitlyn quickly nodded, too.

"This new album has to be really good," Shane went on. "There's a lot of pressure now."

Connect Three's latest album had recently gone platinum. Everyone was thrilled, but Mitchie knew Shane was concerned about the band's follow-up effort.

Shane leaned down to open his guitar case. "Our producer is all over us about making this CD special."

Just then, Lola Scott walked over and sat on the floor. Lola was a veteran at Camp Rock. Not only had she been singing since she was a little girl, her mother was a big-time Broadway star. Lola had inherited her talent and flare. Now she looked up at Shane as he tuned his guitar. "Are you going to play next?"

Shane nodded his head. "Yeah, we're heading back into the studio pretty soon, and I have to finish some songs," he said. "I was hoping that you guys would be my first audience."

Trying to hide her excitement, Lola nodded her head yes. Who wouldn't want to be the first to hear a Shane Gray original?

"Is it about camp?" Caitlyn asked. She leaned forward in her seat, wanting to get the full scoop.

"Kinda," Shane replied mysteriously. "I guess you could say that I have been heavily influenced here." He looked over at Mitchie and smiled.

"Ooooh!" Lola cried, seeing how Shane looked at Michie. "Is it a love song?"

Mitchie pushed Lola with her feet. "Lola!" she scolded, feeling her face turn a beet red.

Shane just laughed. "No! No! It's simpler than that. It's about the summer nights here at camp."

"You mean the superhot summer nights that are going to cause us all to dehydrate?" Caitlyn asked. She began using her hand as a fan. "This heat is killing me!"

Lola took a sip of her ice water. "It's supposed to break tomorrow," she said. "But first we have to make it through tonight!"

"I still can't believe there is no air-conditioning here," Tess said, once again inserting herself into the conversation. Lorraine and Ella were right behind her, holding matching ice-cream cones. All three had one of their hands on their hips, their glossy lips pouting. "This is just not humane. I'm melting!"

"Didn't a certain witch say that?" Caitlyn asked Mitchie.

Mitchie stifled a giggle with her hand as Tess spun and turned away. "Good one, Caitlyn," she threw back over her shoulder.

"Aw, come on," Lola said, laughing. "It isn't so bad. It's camp, people!"

Mitchie nodded her head, smiling. She really liked Lola. She always told the truth and was very straightforward. They had grown closer since the beginning of the summer, and Mitchie was glad.

"Lola's right," Shane chimed in. "Plus, where else would you hear crickets like this?" He gestured toward the three open windows behind the couches. "Isn't that a cool sound?"

Mitchie smiled. The old Shane would never have noticed that! She was glad that he was feeling more relaxed now that Second Session was well under way. He might still occassionally miss the glamorous A-list life, but he definitely knew how to enjoy the peaceful lakeside camp.

"It's great background for a song, don't you think?" Shane said as he tapped his guitar to the cricket beat.

Just then, Brown and the others stopped playing, and the cricket chorus grew even louder.

"You should lay that down as a track on your new CD," Mitchie joked. "Then it would have something special—a Camp Rock tribute."

Standing up, Shane walked over to the window. He turned and looked around the room. A smile spread across his face. "That's an amazing idea," he said. "Mitchie, you're brilliant!"

"What's brilliant?" Peggy asked, joining the group. Now that her set with Brown and the boys was over, she was ready to have a frozen treat with her friends. "The song that we just sang?" She winked at Barron and Sander and did a little curtsy. Ever since Peggy had won Final Jam and stopped being Tess's backup singer, she had been enjoying singing on her own. She loved being a solo vocalist, but jamming with Brown, Sander, and Colby was fun, too.

"You sounded great," Lola told Peggy. "But I don't think Shane was talking about that song. He seems to have some other idea in his head."

Shane ran back over to the couch and packed up his guitar. After he snapped the case shut, he turned to Mitchie.

"Seriously, Mitchie," he said. "Thank you for saving me!" Turning, he dashed out the door with no further explanation.

"What did I miss?" Peggy asked, totally bewildered.

"I have no idea," Mitchie confessed. What had she said to inspire Shane? And when would they hear his new song?

CHAPTER TWO

When Mitchie's alarm rang the next morning, she rolled over and slammed her hand down on the snooze bar. Five minutes later the alarm reminded her that it really was time to haul her body out of bed. Pulling her pillow over her head, Mitchie tried to drown out the buzzing sound. But there was no denying the fact that she had to get up. At least it's not so hot today, she thought as she dragged herself out of bed. The cabin felt significantly cooler, and the breeze coming through the bunk's open windows was crisp.

Part of staying at Camp Rock meant Mitchie still had to work with her mom in the kitchen. Being the cook for the camp was a huge responsibility. Even though she had other kitchen staff, Connie Torres still needed Mitchie's help. The morning shift was usually the hardest one for Mitchie to manage. She had to get up an hour before the rest of the kids. But it was worth it to stay at camp. Quickly pulling on some clothes, she ran down the path to the kitchen.

Her mom was already inside, putting trays of banana muffins in the oven. "Good morning, sleepyhead!" Connie called. "I was wondering if I was going to have to come and pull you out of bed."

Mitchie stretched and pulled her apron off the hook behind the door. "I'm here, I'm here," she said. She rubbed her eyes and yawned. "I may not be totally awake, but I'm here."

"Well, it seems that some people have already gotten an early start today," her mom told her. "Brown, Dee, Shane, and a few of the counselors are huddled at a table in the mess hall. They're working on some big program for today. They've already been through one pot of coffee and a kettle of tea."

Mitchie took a container of blueberries and mixed them into the pancake batter her mom had left on the counter. "Really?" Mitchie asked. The whole camp knew Shane was not a morning person. He could barely manage to get to breakfast on time. "Did they mention what they're doing?"

Her mother shook her head. "No, they just asked for banana muffins and the caffeine. Not sure what they are plotting for you kids today."

Stirring the lumpy batter, Mitchie considered what they might be doing. To get all those people up before breakfast it had to be pretty big.

"Well, whatever the're cooking up," Connie said, "it won't be as delicious as my blueberry pancakes and banana muffins, now will it?" She smiled and gave Mitchie a hug.

Mitchie grinned and spooned the batter onto the hot griddle. She watched for the little bubbles to appear. "No one beats your pancakes, Mom."

"Ah, thanks," Connie said. "I hope everyone feels that way."

"Well, I'm not just saying that because I'm your daughter," Mitchie teased. Usually it was her mom saying things like that. It was fun to switch roles and throw it back on her.

"Come on," Connie told her. "We've got a lot to do here before the rest of the camp gets up." She playfully flicked a dish towel at Mitchie.

After the pancakes and muffins were

finished and Mitchie had set bowls of fresh fruit on each of the tables, she went and sat down to wait for her friends to arrive.

Lola and Caitlyn walked into the mess hall first. Lola plucked a handful of grapes from the fruit bowl at the head of the table and sat down next to Mitchie. "Good morning, sunshine!"

Mitchie smiled but didn't turn. Her eyes were fixed on the table in the front of the mess hall, where Shane, Dee, Brown, and a few of the other counselors were sitting.

"So, any word on what Shane was talking about last night?" Caitlyn asked as she slid onto the bench on the other side of Mitchie. When Mitchie didn't answer, Caitlyn followed her friend's gaze. Immediately, she saw what Mitchie was focusing on. "Or what that big powwow over there is about?" she asked, a teasing tone to her voice.

"Nope," Mitchie said, her eyes still locked on Shane's table. "But it's got to be good.

They've been holed up there since before I arrived."

"Anybody here know how to read lips?" Lola joked.

The girls shrugged. "I guess we'll just have to wait," Mitchie said, giving a little sigh. Dragging her attention away, she peeled a banana and sliced it up, putting it on her pancakes.

"Well, I bet you're right, Mitchie. Whatever they're talking about, it's probably something good," Caitlyn said. She reached for a banana, too, and as she peeled back the skin, nodded her head. "Second Session is always full of good surprises."

"I feel like we already got one today," Lola said. She grinned at her two friends.

Caitlyn looked over and raised an eyebrow. "What are you so happy about?" Caitlyn asked.

"I didn't wake up feeling like I slept in a sauna!" Lola cheered. "It's finally a normal temperature!"

"That's definitely a reason to smile!" Peggy said as she walked over and sat down across from Mitchie. "Hey, M, you talk to Shane yet? What was his deal last night?"

Mitchie shook her head. "No, but Brown is about to make morning announcements, so maybe we'll find out." The girls looked around. Almost all the campers had trickled in and taken their seats. The morning was about to get officially under way.

"Hey, maybe it's the musical mystery!" Lola exclaimed with her eyes wide. "I totally love that!"

Peggy's mouth was now full of blueberry pancakes, but she nodded energetically.

Mitchie looked at them and then at Caitlyn. "What's a musical mystery?"

"Only one of the coolest activities of the summer," Lola answered.

"With an amazing grand prize," Peggy added. "Last year the winning team went on a VIP tour of a recording studio." She dug her fork back into the pancakes. "Man, these are really good! You guys have to have some."

Caitlyn grabbed a plate. "How cool would that be if Connect Three had something to do with the prize?" she asked, reaching across Peggy for the tray of pancakes.

Lola's eyes grew wider. "Mitchie! You'd have to win! If you did, there's no way Shane would not make sure the prize was rockin'!"

"Well, I . . ." Mitchie felt flustered. Even though the heat wave seemed to be over, her face was suddenly burning up. She wanted to dive under the table and hide. "I haven't even won a jam yet. Who says that I can win this mystery thing?"

Caitlyn tapped her arm and winked. "No worries. With me as your partner, you might have a chance!" she told her.

Mitchie wanted to point out that they didn't even know if that was what the big deal was, but at that moment, Brown stood up and walked over to the microphone at the front of the room. "Good morning, Camp Rock!" he cried.

Everyone in the room answered his call with a loud, "Good morning!"

"Thankfully, the heat wave is over," he announced. "But that doesn't mean that we don't have some of the hottest programs of the summer coming up." He smiled at his own clever wording. "And I'm excited to announce that one of those begins today. Today is the annual musical-mystery hunt!"

A loud cheer filled the room, and everyone popped out of their seats.

"Shane is totally involved in this!" Caitlyn said to Mitchie. "Look at him!"

Mitchie turned and saw Shane. Caitlyn seemed to be right. He was beaming with pride. Mitchie pursed her lips. She still wasn't sure what all this had to do with him. Why would he be involved in this particular activity? Returning her attention to Brown, she waited to see what he had to add.

"Okay, settle down," Brown said to the campers. "Let me explain for those of you who are new to Camp Rock. The annual musical mystery is like a scavenger hunt, only we use music for the clues. You work in teams of two—which you can choose. And it's always a highlight with great prizes. And this year is no exception. . . ."

CHAPTER THREE

Absolute silence filled the mess hall as everyone waited for Brown to announce the prize. The room, which was usually loud and full of the sounds of the clattering of dishes and silverware, was completely quiet.

"Oh, the suspense is killing me!" Peggy whispered anxiously.

"Come on Brown!" Lola called out. "Just tell us already!"

Brown took another moment to look around the room. He loved drawing out the suspense almost as much as he loved telling stories about the famous bands he'd worked with. "The grand-prize winners," he finally said, "will get to perform a hidden track—on Connect Three's new CD!" Brown smiled as everyone cheered. "I think that this is a great motivation to win the mystery, and we're thankful to Shane Gray for coming up with the idea."

Brown tried to make a few more announcements, but it was useless. The room was abuzz. At their table, Caitlyn turned to her friends. "Wow, this totally beats last year's tour of the recording studio!"

"This is so amazing," Peggy said, grinning. "I always loved the musical mystery, but this year the prize is extrasweet." She looked over at Tess, who was lecturing Lorraine and Ella. I'm glad this year I don't have to be on Tess's team, Peggy thought. This year, I can do what

I want, how I want. She glanced over at Lola. And maybe I can convince Lola to team up with me. I bet we'd work well together.

At her table, Tess was already plotting. "There is no question. Shane *has* to pick me," Tess said, tossing her stick-straight blond hair. "I would be perfect for a bonus track. I have the talent and the star quality all in one package."

Ella applied her ultrasheer pink gloss and nodded in agreement. "Totally," she said. "Talent and star quality."

Lorraine cocked her head. She hated to contradict Tess but . . . "Don't you have to *win* the musical mystery hunt to get on the CD?" she asked.

"Whatever," Tess said, getting up from the table. She waved her hand as though the details didn't matter. "It's Shane's CD. He should have some say in who gets to sing, no matter who wins."

"Mitchie, I'm telling you, if it is Shane's

choice, then you have the gig totally sealed," Lola said in a separate—but almost identical—discussion taking place back at Mitchie's table. "There's no way Shane wouldn't pick you." At that moment, she felt a bit jealous of her friend. She hung her head and hoped it didn't show.

Mitchie looked at her friends who were all staring at her. "You guys, its Shane's CD," she said. "But Brown just said that the *winner* of the musical-mystery hunt is who gets to sing on the track. Not just who Shane *feels* like having sing."

"Mitchie's right," Caitlyn said, giving her friend a reassuring look. "He doesn't get to pick. It's the winner of the hunt. Fair and square."

Tess had gotten up for juice and overheard the last part of their conversation. "We'll see about that," she said. "I have a feeling that this hunt is going to be different from all others."

Mitchie had to admit that she was kind of bummed out. It would have been nice if Shane had simply asked her to sing on his CD. But when she looked around at all the excitement that Brown's announcement had created, she knew why Shane had made his decision. The whole dining hall was still buzzing, and Mitchie had a feeling that this was going to be the most competitive musical mystery hunt Camp Rock had ever had.

CHAPTER FOUR

"**H**ey, girls! Thanks so much for helping out," Dee said to Mitchie and Caitlyn later that morning as they walked into Keynote.

Looking around, the girls mouths dropped open. The place was a mess! There were stacks of rainbow-colored CD cases and tall piles of white envelopes spread across the floor. Normally, the cabin was used for practicing songs or dance moves, but today it was musical-mystery headquarters.

"I don't think that we would have gotten this all done by the afternoon if you hadn't volunteered to help us out," Dee added. Her usually cheerful expression looked a bit haggard.

"We're happy to help," Mitchie said. Which was true. They had free time on their hands, which they hadn't expected. .

Usually, she and Caitlyn would have been in the kitchen. Even though Caitlyn's kitchen-duty punishment for a minor food fight had ended after the first session, she still came back often to hang out with Mitchie and her mom. But lunch that day was a cookout, and there wasn't much prep work needed. Connie had explained that Dee was stressed out about getting everything ready for the musical mystery. She had suggested the girls go help her instead, and they had happily agreed.

Even though she ran the mystery hunt

each year, Dee liked to keep the clues new and fresh—and that usually meant waiting till the last minute to organize everything. This summer was no exception!

As soon as Mitchie eyed the piles stacked around Keynote, she realized why her mom had sent them. The hunt was supposed to start after lunch, but from the look of things that wasn't going to happen. "What do you need us to do?" Mitchie asked.

Dee pointed to the CD cases and the envelopes. "We need to have each clue in the right case. They are all color-coordinated." She held up an envelope that had a blue dot in the lower right-hand corner. "See, this one goes in a blue case."

"So each team will be a different color? Very clever," Mitchie said. She sat down on the floor in front of a stack of cases and envelopes.

"Yes," Dee answered. "Because there are just too many campers, there *will* be a few different teams with the same color. But I don't think that will be a problem. I make it so all the clues are the same—just in a different order. That way everyone isn't running to the same clue at the same time. *But* everyone will end up together at the final one."

"Which is always the hardest one!" Caitlyn exclaimed.

Dee laughed. "Well, we have to keep you on your toes!"

The two friends sat down next to her and began sorting through the colored cases. "This shouldn't be too bad," Mitchie said, trying to sound optimistic.

"It seemed like a great idea," Dee said, sighing. "But we just decided to do the hunt this morning, so it's been hard to get every-thing organized."

"No sneaking peeks at the clues," Shane said, coming into the room. He winked at Mitchie as he took a stack of the envelopes and cases. "I'll be watching you!"

"Very funny," Mitchie said, laughing. She held up one of the envelopes. "Look, the clues are sealed. No cheaters, no worries."

Shane laughed. "I used to have a blast with the hunt," he said. "I'm sure this year's is going to be the best yet."

"And you're not saying that just because the prize is singing on your new CD, right?" Mitchie said, teasing Shane. She began to put the yellow-dotted envelopes in yellow cases.

Shane reached over and tugged playfully at Mitchie's hair. "Yeah, yeah," he said. "Say what you will, but the truth is I think that this track is going to help Connect Three more than people realize."

Mitchie and Caitlyn raised their eyebrows in disbelief.

"Seriously," Shane went on to explain. "To create a CD with bonus tracks that are cool is really hard to do! Our producers are after us to get some material that will be exciting and cutting edge. And that's what Camp Rock is all about."

"That's what I love to hear!" Brown said as he walked into the cabin. He was beaming. "And with this prize, everyone wins, and that's what I like to see."

"Well, technically, not everyone," Caitlyn said softly. "But we are sure going to try, right Mitchie?"

"You bet!" Mitchie exclaimed. "Bring it on! We're so ready."

Shane laughed. "All right, let's see how you do. This year the clues are hard—and a little tricky."

Looking over at Caitlyn, Mitchie smiled. "I think we can handle the pressure. Just you wait."

Soon all the clues were safely tucked into the right cases and ready to be placed around camp. That job was reserved for Dee. Caitlyn and Mitchie went off to a salsa class, which was being held at the stage by the lake. It was a beautiful, slightly cooler day, and it was nice to be outside dancing.

"Hey, are you going to be partners for the hunt?" Lola asked when she saw Mitchie and Caitlyn. She turned her head and smiled at Peggy. "I've teamed up with Ms. Margaret Dupree."

Peggy laughed when Lola used her "stage name." At Final Jam, she had debuted her full name. She had wanted to hide the fact that she was performing for the first time as a solo vocalist instead of as one of Tess's backup singers for as long as possible. Hearing Lola call her that now brought back fond memories.

When their dance instructor, a pretty brunette named Jessie, cued the music, they all stopped talking and focused on the routine.

They were in the middle of a particularly hard part of the dance when Dee appeared on the side of the stage. Calling Jessie over, the two spoke in hushed tones. Then Jessie called Lola over.

"What's going on?" Caitlyn asked as Lola quickly gathered her things.

Lola shrugged. "I have no idea," she said. "I guess I'll find out."

"I hope everything's okay," Peggy said. "Come find us after," she told her. "We'll be here by the lake, okay?"

Lola agreed and quickly walked over to Dee. Her heart was racing as she followed Dee away from the lake and down the path heading toward the office. Turning, Dee noticed Lola's pale face. "Oh, don't worry, honey," she reassured her. "You just have a phone call. Shouldn't be anything to get all worked up about. I promise."

Lola breathed a sigh of relief. Doreen, the camp receptionist, looked up from her desk as she entered the office. As usual, the receptionist's white hair was tied up in a bun at her neck. She'd been working there forever and was like an unofficial grandmother to everyone at camp.

"It's Giselle," Doreen told her. "She says it's urgent. You can use that phone over there." She pointed to the far desk by the window. "She's on line two."

Not sure why her mother's personal assistant would be calling her, Lola grabbed the phone. Giselle never called her at camp. "Hello?" she said tentatively.

"Hey, babe," Giselle cooed in her raspy voice. "Listen honey, your mom wanted me to call you to tell you . . ." Then there was a static break that cracked over the phone line.

"Tell me what?" Lola cried. "Is she all right?" She could just imagine Giselle doing three or four things as she chatted on her headset. While her mom was not a supermega star like Tess's mother, she was still a major Broadway actress who needed someone like Giselle to keep her schedule straight.

"Yes, yes, she's perfectly fine," Giselle finally answered.

Her voice sounded far away, and it was

difficult to hear what she was saying. Lola strained to listen, but she only got part of what was said. ". . . need to come home."

"What?" Lola shouted. She held her breath as she waited to hear Giselle's response. Of all the times to get a bad cell phone connection! "I need to come home? Wait! Why?"

Doreen looked up from the papers on her desk, and Lola turned her back to look out the window. She took a deep breath and willed herself not to cry. "Giselle, what's going on?" Lola asked. "Can I talk to my mother?"

"Babe, this is a bad connection, I'm sorry." Giselle's voice continued to cut in and out. "Your mom is doing a show right now."

Lola bit her lip as she listened to Giselle motor on. Normally, any phone calls she received during camp were from her mother directly. This all felt a bit strange. Lola started to bite her nails.

"Everything is *okay*," Giselle said. "No one's hurt or sick. Just tired. We'll try you after the show tonight. Maybe the line will be clearer."

With that, Giselle hung up. Lola stared at the receiver in her hand. Despite Giselle's reassurances, it didn't feel like everything was all right. Giselle had said something about coming home. Was Lola going to have to leave camp? Tears started to run from her eyes. Her head was spinning. She didn't know how to react, but she *did* know that if she had to leave Camp Rock early, she would be devastated.

She took a deep breath and slowly placed the receiver back on the phone base.

"Lola, is everything okay?" Doreen asked.

Lola turned around to see Doreen's worried expression.

"I'm not really sure," Lola responded as she slowly walked to the front door. In a daze, she walked back down to the lake.

The salsa class was over, and Lola found her friends all hanging out under a tree by the water.

"Hey, are you okay?" Mitchie called when she spotted Lola. She, Caitlyn, and Peggy ran up to meet her. "What happened?"

"I think I may have to leave camp early," Lola said, trying not to cry as soon as she said the words out loud. Camp Rock meant everything to her. For her mom to pull her away now, something must be seriously wrong.

"Oh, Lola!" her friends cried.

"Well, you're not leaving today, right?" Peggy said, trying to cheer her up. Lola shrugged. She didn't know. But optimistic as always, Peggy persevered. "You can't leave. You and I are going to win this year's musical mystery!"

Lola smiled at her friends. They were right. She didn't want to think about leaving right now. There was the grand prize of singing on a Connect Three CD that she wanted to collect. If anything could cheer her up, that was it. She joined her friends as they walked toward the beach where the lunch barbecue was set up.

She would just have to try and figure out Giselle's cryptic message later.

CHAPTER FIVE

The line for hamburgers was long by the time the four friends arrived, and Mitchie fanned herself with her plate as she waited. "I know that the heat wave has broken, but it is still so hot!"

"Well, not as hot as it was last night," Caitlyn said. "This is just normal hot. At least we aren't going to dehydrate."

"Speak for yourself," Colby said as he

joined his friends on the line. "I'm ready to take a dive in the water." He strained his neck to look over the crowd. "But first I have to get one of those burgers. They smell so good."

"Nothing beats a burger," Barron said from his place in line ahead of Colby. "And the whole outdoor thing just makes it better."

"Let's move along, people," Sander added. He was standing next to Barron, eager for his lunch.

"Are you two going to be partners for the musical-mystery hunt?" Mitchie asked. It was no secret that Barron and Sander were a great musical team.

"You bet," Sander said. He leaned in closer to Mitchie. "So you better watch your back!"

Mitchie laughed. "Well, I've been warned," she said. "But you should know, Caitlyn and I want to win pretty badly."

"And so do we," Peggy chimed in. "Lola

and I are a perfect team. Not only do we harmonize together, we are going to rock this hunt to first place!" She grabbed Lola's hand and raised it above her head like a champion.

Lola appreciated Peggy's enthusiasm, but she still couldn't take her mind off the phone call from Giselle. How could her mom expect her to just sit tight without any explanation? She didn't know if she could wait until tonight to find out what was going wrong. The suspense was totally going to get to her.

Seeing the expression on Lola's face, Mitchie realized that her friend was thinking about the phone call. She turned to Lola and put a hand on her shoulder. "Don't worry, Lola. I'm sure everything is going to be okay. There's nothing we can do for the moment, so you just need to enjoy being here now!"

"Plus, I need you as my partner," Peggy added, putting her arm around her. She gave Lola a tight squeeze. "I'm sure tonight when you talk to your mom, she'll explain everything and you'll feel better. The musical mystery is going to start any minute, and we're going to win!"

Lola nodded her head. She looked around at her friends. They were right. She didn't want to miss out on the musical-mystery hunt. This was an event she had been looking forward to all summer. Her competitive spirit started to kick in. "You're right," she said. Then she smiled at Peggy. "You know, I came in second last year."

"I remember!" Peggy said, grinning. "You really wanted that tour of the recording studio. Too bad that Liz Randell got that lyric seconds before you!"

"Liz got to go to the recording studio?" Mitchie asked. She looked over at the brown-haired girl sitting with a bunch of people on the lawn. "That's awesome."

"But she didn't get to record a track that would be on a best-selling CD like this year,"

Lola said, already starting to feel a bit better. "You're right. I have to wait to talk to my mom tonight. In the meantime, I'm all about winning this prize."

Tess noticed the girls chatting and strolled up to them, just as Lola was talking about the hunt. "I wouldn't count on winning that prize," she said, flipping her blond hair. If there was a prize to win, Tess wanted it.

"Tess, who are you teaming up with?" Mitchie asked, trying to be friendly.

Tess stood with her hands on her hips. "We just got permission to be a threesome," Tess said. As if on cue, Ella and Lorraine appeared at her side wearing matching bright pink lip gloss. "We're a tight group, you know." She flashed Peggy a stone-cold look and then waltzed over to grab a veggie burger.

"I doubt those three heads are going to be better than any of our two," Caitlyn mumbled.

Mitchie shrugged. "You never know. Tess

always has her eye on the prize, and she is a fierce competitor. We're going to have to be at the top of our game."

"Oh, for sure," Peggy said. "Singing on a CD? I think it's the best prize ever for a musical mystery. It's golden."

"Maybe even platinum!" Caitlyn said with a wink.

The line started to move, and all the campers eventually got their burgers, chips, and juice. They sat in the shade, eating. Then Dee got up and explained some ground rules for the musical mystery.

"We have color-coded all the clues so that each team will look for their color CD case," Dee explained. "Even though there are a few teams with the same color, each team of two will be judged separately." She looked around at all the campers. "At each location, you will find a clue that will lead to the next one. The clues are in a different order, so please do not share any information with other campers as you work your way through to the end."

"Wow," Mitchie whispered to Caitlyn. "This is going to be a lot of fun. Dee and the staff put a ton of work into this."

"Oh, Dee takes a lot of pride in this hunt," Caitlyn responded. "She works really hard on all the clues. You'll see—it's not easy! We're going to have to work together to get them all."

"You are allowed to use any musical instruments in camp to help you figure out any clue," Dee went on. "Except your own personal ones. All bunks are off-limits for the afternoon."

There was a groan from the crowd. Dee put her hand up for quiet, and then continued her instructions. "Every clue is about music—all parts of music, from lyrics to tempo and style. The clues will all lead you to a place on camp where you'll find your next clue until the mystery is solved."

Brown stood up next to Dee. "Some clues are not as obvious as others," he advised. "So stay focused."

"Let's start!" someone yelled from the crowd.

"All right!" Dee said. "Please stand with your partner, and the staff will hand out the first clues. Use the stickers inside the case to put on your shirt so the counselors at each spot know your team color."

Mitchie jumped up. She was so excited. Clasping her hands together, she noticed Shane walking with Brown toward Dee to help give out the clues.

"There are five clues in total," Dee added. "Have fun and play fair! Enjoy the musical mystery!"

Everyone cheered, ready for the event to begin. Dee, Brown, Shane, and the other counselors handed out the clues. Mitchie put on her blue sticker and handed the other to Caitlyn. The two girls moved a bit away from the others before Mitchie opened the first clue. She stared at the musical notes on the sheet. "It's sheet music," she said to Caitlyn, confused.

Caitlyn laughed. "Yes, and the trick is to find out quickly what the song is so we can figure out where the next clue is." She grabbed the sheet and started humming the notes on the page. The tune didn't sound familiar to her, and she started to panic. When she looked over at Mitchie, she was humming the tune as well. "Do you know this song?" she asked, full of hope.

Mitchie knew she had heard the tune before. But where? She racked her brain, trying to remember *when*. Caitlyn hummed it again. When Caitlyn was finished, she looked up at Mitchie. All the teams were huddled together, trying to figure out their clues. They had to hurry!

"Wait, I do know it!" Mitchie exclaimed. It was at the tip of her tongue. "I'm pretty sure that my dad has it on his iPod. Hum it one more time."

Humming the tune again, Caitlyn hoped that Mitchie's brain would retrieve the information quickly. Some of the other campers had obviously figured out their clues. They were already racing to their next spot. Reading the notes carefully, she finished humming and looked at her friend expectantly. "Well?"

"Sittin' on the Dock of the Bay!" Mitchie exclaimed. "It's an Otis Redding song."

"Perfect!" Caitlyn cried, giving Mitchie a hug. Then she lowered her voice so she wouldn't give away the clue. "So, our next clue should be at the dock. Great work, Mitchie!" They traded high fives and the two ran toward the boat dock.

Mitchie felt bad for all the times she'd complained about her dad plugging in his iPod in the car. His musical taste had solved the first clue. She was hopeful that there would be more songs she would recognize to help put her and Caitlyn in first place.

Peggy and Lola and Sander and Barron had run off to the kitchen with their song clue. And Tess was already stomping around, annoyed that her clue proved to be a song that was not familiar to her, Ella, or Lorraine. Everyone at Camp Rock was on a quest to solve the musical mystery—and get the grand prize.

CHAPTER Six

When Mitchie and Caitlyn arrived at the dock, they found a counselor sitting with his feet dangling in the water. He was there to watch the large stack of CD cases and make sure everyone played fair and took their own color.

"Hey, there," Caitlyn said, slightly out of breath. She pointed to the blue sticker on her shirt. "Team blue, here," she said to him.

The tall, blond counselor handed Caitlyn the blue CD case and smiled. "Good luck," he said and then turned his face back to the sun. He definitely had one of the best spots in the hunt to work on his tan.

"Thanks," Caitlyn said. She quickly opened the case and took out the envelope hidden inside.

"Is it another piece of sheet music?" Mitchie asked eagerly. She followed Caitlyn over to the shade of an old tree to examine their clue.

Caitlyn made a face as she studied the paper. "Yes, but I need a piano," she said. "I can't make this melody out without an instrument. It's a bit more complicated."

"Here, let me try," Mitchie said, taking the paper. She tried to hum the first few bars, but it was a harder piece of music to hum than their first clue. She glanced up at Caitlyn. "You're right. Where's the closest piano?" she asked, looking around. Luckily, there were plenty of pianos at camp. They just had to find the nearest one—and fast.

"Keynote," Caitlyn said with confidence. "Let's go!"

Both girls took off, racing up the hill to Keynote. A few hours ago the cabin had been the headquarters for the musical mystery. Now it was part of the game.

When they ran through the door, Mitchie and Caitlyn looked around. Two pianos and a fan guitar were set up so that the campers could use them to figure out clues. A counselor was sitting in the corner of the room to keep an eye on things. A few teams were already there trying to sound out their clues.

Caitlyn slipped into the seat in front of one of the pianos just as Barron, Sander, and Tess and her entourage entered the room. Barely sparing them a glance, Caitlyn placed the sheet music on the piano. Then, using the soft pedal to muffle the sound, she lightly tapped the keys. She didn't want anyone in the cabin with the same clue to hear the melody and figure it out first.

"Could you please hurry it up?" Tess said, directing her glare at Caitlyn. "We don't have all day here."

"Yeah," Ella added. "Hurry up."

Lorraine flipped her hair, which got stuck on her glossy lips, and tried to maintain the same sour expression that Tess had on her face. Mitchie tried not to giggle. She knew Lorraine was a really sweet girl. The sour act was being displayed just to try and fit in with Tess.

"Don't pay attention to them," Caitlyn told Mitchie. "Remember, the clues are spaced so that no one has the same one at the same time. They probably don't have ours. But we should still keep our discovery quiet, so lean in close."

Mitchie moved in closer to the piano, listening carefully to the melody Caitlyn was playing. It was vaguely familiar. Mitchie started to jump up and down. "I know it!" she said, clapping her hands excitedly. "I totally know it!"

"Well, then give up the piano," Tess ordered from the corner.

Ella reapplied her lip gloss and handed it to Tess. "You want some?"

Tess pushed the pot of gloss away. "What I want is to know what our song is so Caitlyn better get a move on," she snapped.

Caitlyn ignored Tess and looked up at Mitchie. "Are you sure?" she asked.

"Totally," Mitchie said. "I'm loving this game! Let's get out of here, and I'll tell you."

Tess waltzed over to their piano. "Um, yeah, moving sometime today would be nice," she said, forcing an insincere smile.

"Hold your horses," Caitlyn said as she stood up. She collected her sheet-music clue and her CD case. "Everyone gets a turn." Then she made a royal sweeping motion toward the piano with her arm as she passed. "The piano is all yours, Your Majesty."

"Whatever," Tess said as she sat down. "Ella, give me the song!" she barked.

Mitchie and Caitlyn ran out of the cabin, leaving Tess to throw one of her fits. When they were safely away from the other campers, Mitchie turned to Caitlyn. "That's a Rod Rock song!" she exclaimed. "It was a little hard to figure out, but I am totally sure. I just can't remember the words."

Now that Mitchie mentioned it, Caitlyn recognized the melody. How could she not have? The song was hugely popular last year—especially around July Fourth. "You're really good at this game, Mitchie!" Caitlyn gave her another high five. Then her expression changed. Figuring out the song was only half the answer. They had to know where to find the next clue and that meant knowing the words or at least the title. "So, where is the song telling us to go?"

Mitchie started to remember some of the words, and they began to piece the song together. When they got to the lyric that had the word *flagpole*, they had it.

"That's it!" Caitlyn shouted. There most definitely was a flagpole at Camp Rock, and she was sure it was where their next clue would be waiting. "We've got to hurry!"

Once again, the two girls ran across camp. As they hurried, they spotted their friends all scurrying around as well. This was turning out to be a fierce competition.

Reaching the clearing near the flagpole, Mitchie looked over and saw a circle of chairs set up in the center of camp. Shane was lounging in one of them, next to Brown.

"Shane is loving this, don't you think?" Mitchie asked Caitlyn. "He just gets to sit back and see who wins."

"Well, hopefully, it will be us!" Caitlyn said, giving her partner a wink.

Mitchie reached the flagpole first and

took the blue CD case. Inside was another clue—a sheet of lyrics without music!

"Oh, great," Caitlyn moaned. "What are we supposed to do without this?"

Before Mitchie could answer, Colby and Andy came over to them.

"Hey, how are you guys doing?" Colby asked.

"Good," Mitchie said, trying not to look too deflated. They had been doing well—until now. But no way was she giving up hope, yet. And she didn't want to give away any indication that they had just gotten a clue that stumped them. "We're on number three. What about you?" she said with a smile on her face.

Andy grinned. "Number four! Better step up your game, Torres!"

Colby pumped his fist in the air. "We are the champions, my friends!" he cried out confidently.

"Oh, I wouldn't start gloating now," Caitlyn

scolded. "It's not over till it's over."

The boys laughed. "See you later, gators," they called as they ran off.

Mitchie and Caitlyn looked at each other in a panic. How had Colby and Andy gotten to the fourth clue so quickly?

"All right," Caitlyn said calmly when the boys were gone. "We can figure this out."

Mitchie wasn't so sure. "Maybe if we say the words out loud, it will help."

Willing to try, Caitlyn started reading the lyrics. When she got to the chorus, Mitchie raised her eyes. "Oh, I don't believe it."

"What?" Caitlyn said, leaning forward. "Who wrote this? Is it like ancient music or what?"

"It's the Beach Boys!" Mitchie exclaimed. "I should have known that if my dad's music was part of this, my mom would have to be in on the action as well." She shook her head. "My mom loves the Beach Boys. It's, like, old surfer music."

"Well, let's hear it for your mom!" Caitlyn cheered. "I guess we're heading back to the lake. If I had to bet, I'd say there's a clue at the lifeguard chair."

Together, they broke into a sprint. If they were going to start gaining on the competition, they would need to stay on track and move faster.

CHAPTER SEVEN

Mitchie and Caitlyn weren't the only ones hot on the trail. Lola and Peggy had gotten to the dock and were tearing open their clue just as Tess, Ella, and Lorraine appeared.

"We're on our third clue, what about you?" Tess asked, using her envelope to fan her face.

"Yeah, our third," Ella repeated. The scavenger hunt hadn't stopped Ella from dressing to impress. She wore pink flip-flops that matched her pink tank top and pink lip gloss. And in her dark hair she had a simple pink headband. She looked more ready for a day on a yacht than a scavenger hunt in the woods.

"Oh, we have every intention of beating you and everyone else," Peggy responded. She hugged the next clue close to her chest. "You are not going to win this one, Tess."

Tess gave Peggy and Lola a long look that went from head to toe. "I wouldn't be so sure of that," she said. Then she waved her hand as if she were shooing Lola away. "Shouldn't you be off crying somewhere about going home?" she taunted. "I hear you're leaving us shortly."

Peggy couldn't believe it. How had Tess found out? And how was it any of her business? She was about to say something to that effect, but she didn't have to. Lola was perfectly capable of handling the situation.

Staring Tess right in the eye, Lola kept her voice calm and level. "I wouldn't bank on that, Tess. And if you think you are going to psych me out of winning today, you have another thing coming."

Tess shrugged her shoulders and picked up her orange CD. With no more disses to deliver, she took off; Ella and Lorraine were close behind her.

"I guess bad news travels fast, huh?" Peggy said, when the other girls were out of earshot.

"It sure does," Lola said. Even though she had shown a brave face to Tess, Lola was not that confident. The phone call was still weighing heavily on her, making it hard to keep her head in the game.

"Look at it this way," Peggy said, noticing Lola's gloomy expression. "Clearly, Tess sees your leaving as good news. She'd love to have one less person to compete against. Which means she is legitimately nervous that we could win." Peggy smiled encouragingly. "Come on, you don't know for sure that you have anything to be sad about."

"You're right," Lola said, sighing. "I'm not going to let Tess Tyler ruin this hunt. Or our very good chance of winning the grand prize. Come on, Peggy."

Peggy nodded, glad to have her partner back. They opened their next clue and tried to read the notes on the sheet of music. With each step, the clues were getting more challenging. They needed another piano to figure this one out.

"The small rehearsal cabin is a bit farther away than Keynote," Lola said. "But it might be less crowded. And there are pianos there."

That made sense to Peggy, and they quickly headed in that direction. But apparently, they weren't the only ones with that idea. There were two other teams ahead of them when they got there.

"We should probably wait," Peggy said.

"By the time we run back to Keynote, it might be our turn here."

"Plus, there's probably a line at those pianos, too," Lola added.

Having played before, they both knew that half the game was strategy and the other half was getting access to instruments. Last year there had been a big uproar when some of the campers had used electric pianos and other instruments from the bunks. Ultimately, Brown and Dee had decided to ban all access to campers' residences. There were a bunch of counselors making sure that no one tried to cheat. Most campers followed the rules. But that meant the approved instruments were always in high demand.

Peggy and Lola waited anxiously. Finally, one of the teams jumped up and raced out of the small cabin. The counselor keeping order waved at Peggy and Lola to come and begin their turn. Within seconds, Peggy figured out the clue.

"I got it!" she shouted.

A few campers looked over at her, and she lowered her voice. "Let's go," she said to Lola a little more quietly. When they were both outside, Lola turned to her. "Flagpole, right?"

"YES!" Peggy cried. "I thought it was that Rod Rock song, but I wasn't sure till I heard the melody. The flagpole is totally where our next clue is!"

They both ran toward the center of camp. As they reached the flagpole, they saw Mitchie and Caitlyn running toward them.

"Hey!" Mitchie called, waving her hand. "What number are you guys on?"

"We're heading for number four," Peggy said, a big smile on her face.

"Us, too! We just got our third and are heading for four," Caitlyn said with a grin. "This year is tough. Dee stepped up the game, big-time. The clues are really hard to figure out."

"I know," Lola said. "But we're rocking, right, Peggy?"

Peggy winked at her partner. "Oh, yeah!" she cheered. Mitchie and Caitlyn turned to go as Peggy and Lola raced to the base of the flagpole.

Just as they reached the pole, Doreen's voice echoed from the camp loudspeakers.

"Lola Scott, please come to the office. Lola Scott, please come to the office. Thank you." Doreen's voice was clear and concise. Hearing Doreen say her name made Lola's heart stop. She wasn't supposed to hear from her mom until tonight. Something *must* be wrong.

CHAPTER EIGHT

Over the loudspeaker, Lola's name was called yet again. Mitchie and Caitlyn had heard the first announcement and stopped in their tracks. Looking at each other, they had silently agreed—they were turning around. Quickly, they made their way back to Lola and Peggy.

Standing there, even though surrounded by her friends, Lola felt alone and worried.

Peggy saw the look on her friend's face and put an arm around her shoulder.

Lola appreciated Peggy's support, but she felt bad, anyway. She knew this contest was a big deal to Peggy and that she was jeopardizing their chance of winning. Then again, how could she not go see what that call was about?

"What do you think is going on?" Mitchie asked, still panting from their sprint back to the flagpole.

"I'm not sure," Lola said. She hoped with all her heart it wasn't terrible news.

Peggy stepped forward. "Come on, we'll all walk you over to the office and wait for you while you take the call."

Lola looked up at her friends, her brown eyes wide with surprise. "But the musical mystery! What about the prize? You've got to keep moving, people!"

Mitchie smiled. "We're here for you, Lola. Don't worry about the clues. The most important thing right now is finding out what is going on. The game is far from over. So, let's get a move on and go check out that phone call."

Feeling better, Lola followed her friends to the office door. They stood outside, holding their clues while she went in to take her call.

"Listen, you need to keep going," Lola said one more time before she went inside the office. "I'll meet up with you after. I promise."

Her friends didn't move.

"I mean it," she said. "Now scoot! If Tess Tyler goes and wins this contest and not one of us, I'm going to hold you all personally responsible!"

Mitchie, Caitlyn, and Peggy all laughed.

"Are you sure you'll be okay alone?" Peggy asked.

Lola nodded her head. "Yes," she said. "I promise. Now get!" As she turned to open the door, she looked back at her three friends one more time. "And thanks," she said. What she didn't say was that if the news was bad, she would *want* to be alone. She hated crying in front of people—even friends.

Inside, Doreen was sitting at her desk.

"Hi, sweetie," she greeted her. "Your call is on line three."

Slowly, Lola walked over. She wasn't sure what to expect. . . . Who would be on the phone—Giselle or her mother? Lola took a deep breath. Then she picked up the receiver and pressed the button next to the blinking light. "Hello?" she said tentatively.

"Great, you're there!" Giselle's voice boomed. "Hold for your mom."

"Mom?" she cried.

"She'll be right there, Lola," Giselle said. "I'm patching her through now."

Taking a seat on the old wooden swivel chair, Lola waited to hear her mother's voice. Through the window, she could see pairs of campers running to the flagpole, getting their designated clue, and then heading off to the next location. She wondered how Peggy was doing. If she really did have to leave camp early, maybe she could at least leave a winner. Lola sunk down lower in the chair. But she really didn't want to leave camp at all. She bit her nails as she waited, hoping that her worst fears wouldn't come true.

CHAPTER NINE

"**H**ow's it going, songbirds?" Shane called to Mitchie and the others as they walked by. He was still lounging in a chair near the center of camp.

Mitchie jogged over to him. "We're doing okay," she said when she reached Shane. She nodded toward Caitlyn and Peggy who were walking ahead. "We're all off to find our fourth clue. But we had to leave Lola back at the office. She got another phone call, and we're hoping that it's not bad news."

Shane nodded. "Yeah, I heard Doreen call her. I hope she's okay." He lifted his dark sunglasses up onto his forehead. "But if you want to stay in the competition, you need to bust a move, Torres."

"I hear you," Mitchie said. "Believe me, Caitlyn and I want to win. But Lola is our friend."

"And you are definitely a really good one," Shane said, giving her a hug.

Mitchie glowed. She still wasn't used to being friends with a pop star. He was so nice and so cute that sometimes she got frazzled. Trying to act cool, Mitchie smiled. "Okay, off to the lifeguard chair," she said. "Nice addition of the Beach Boys song, by the way. My mother didn't have anything to do with that one, huh?"

Shane laughed. "Well, she *was* singing a Beach Boys tune early this morning when we were desperate for clues. She was incredibly helpful!"

"I knew it," Mitchie said, grinning. "But it's all good. All those times in the car with her and my dad listening to their music has served me well for this competition!" Waving good-bye, she turned and raced off to catch up with Caitlyn and Peggy.

"I hope Lola's okay," Peggy was saying to Caitlyn when Mitchie caught up to them. Peggy's clue was down by the docks, too, so she continued walking with Caitlyn and Mitchie to the lakefront. "She'll be crushed if she has to leave early. Lola loves it here!"

"We *all* love it here," Caitlyn said, looking around at their surroundings. The sun was glistening on the lake, and the trees were swaying in the gentle breeze. She couldn't begin to imagine what it would feel like if she got a call telling her she had to leave camp early. After all, this is what she lived for all year!

Mitchie, Caitlyn, and Peggy were silent, each one lost in her own thoughts about leaving and about why they loved camp. Reaching the waterfront, they parted ways, their expressions glum.

"We'll check back with you before we head to the next clue," Mitchie told Peggy before she left for the dock.

"Okay," Peggy said. "Hopefully, Lola will be back by then."

Caitlyn and Mitchie quickly found their clue under the lifeguard chair—just as Caitlyn had suspected. They both studied the sheet music carefully. In this case, the piece was elaborate, and Mitchie looked up at Caitlyn, stumped.

"What are we supposed to do with this?" she asked, totally bewildered.

Caitlyn stared at the paper. "Wait a minute . . . this is classical music," Caitlyn said. Suddenly she understood what she was looking at.

"Yikes," Mitchie said, still unsure of what the clue meant.

Meanwhile, Caitlyn continued to eye the music. "Dee said that the clue could be in the music, so maybe it's something to do with the notes." She examined the music—it looked as if it could be some kind of sonnet. Then she saw something that made her grin. "I think I got it!" she exclaimed.

"Really?" Mitchie asked. She scanned the music again, wondering what had triggered the clue for Caitlyn. To her, it looked like any other complex composition. "What?"

Caitlyn pointed to the upper left-hand corner. "The whole piece is written in B flat. And the first note is a B note. As in the B-Note canteen!"

"Wow," Mitchie said, impressed that Caitlyn had been able to make that association so quickly.

"Come on," Caitlyn said, already running. "Let's go!"

"And the B-Note is right next to the office so we can check on Lola," Mitchie said.

They both ran quickly, hoping that they'd figure out the next clue as quickly. And maybe hear some good news from Lola regarding the "urgent" call.

CHAPTER
TEN

"Hey, sweetie!"

Lola almost burst into tears when she heard her mother's familiar voice. She sounded completely normal! How could she sound normal when Lola's heart was racing out of control!

"Mom! Are you okay?" Lola asked anxiously. She twisted the old-fashioned phone cord around her finger. "What's going on? Why did Giselle call?"

"Oh, sweetie," Lola's mom cooed, apparently oblivious to her daughter's stressed tone. "It's so great to hear your voice! How's camp? How are you?"

Lola was confused. Her mother sounded fine. She didn't sound like there was some horrible emergency. What was going on? Lola cut to the chase. "Mom, what was Giselle talking about today? Do I have to come home early? Is everything okay?" She couldn't take any more waiting. There was a long pause on the other end, and Lola held her breath. Suddenly it sounded as if her mom was choking—or hiccuping. Her heart beat faster—until she realized her mother was laughing!

"Oh, no!" her mother said. "Sweetie, you got it all wrong! The message was that *I* was coming home early. We decided to cut the summer production short. I'll be home by the end of the week. Since I missed visitor's day,

I was hoping that I could come see you. Maybe I could catch one of your stellar performances I've been hearing so much about."

Lola's mouth dropped open. How could the message have gotten so messed up? She was so relieved that she didn't even know whether to laugh or cry or yell at her mother. "Oh, I'm so happy!" Lola finally managed to say. "I thought something was really wrong and that I was going to have to come home."

"Oh, don't be silly," her mother said. "I know what Camp Rock means to you."

Hearing her mother's assurances made Lola feel so much better. But she wasn't about to drop the topic. "You never should have had Giselle call me like that," she said, relief turning to anger. "Mom, I was really worried that something awful had happened to you."

There was a pause, and Lola could hear her mother exhale. "I'm so, so sorry, love," she said softly. "It's just when I heard the news, I wanted you to know. Giselle did say that it was a bad connection, but I didn't realize how bad. I had no idea that you only got part of the message . . . and the wrong message at that!"

Lola couldn't stay mad. Everything was okay. Her mom would get to come up to camp *and* she didn't have to go anywhere! It was the best news ever.

When she hung up the phone, she went over and gave Doreen a huge bear hug. "I'm staying!" she told her happily.

Doreen looked a little surprised by the affection, but gave Lola a smile. "I'm glad to hear that, dear," she said.

Lola practically skipped out the door. At that moment, she felt like the luckiest person at Camp Rock.

Then she saw a few teams race past her, and she remembered the musical mystery. She would have to do her celebrating later.

Right now she had to catch up with Peggy. The only thing that could make this day even more perfect would be winning the grand prize and singing a track on the next Connect Three album!

CHAPTER
ELEVEN

Mitchie and Caitlyn were jogging to the B-Note when they saw Lola walking out of the office. Changing direction, they took a detour and ran over to her. This was the moment of truth: would their friend have good news—or bad?

They didn't have to wait long to hear it. "I'm staying!" Lola shouted when she saw her friends running toward her. She did a little dance and turned in a circle. "It's *my mother* who's coming home early! Her summer tour was cut short. I can't believe how badly that message got messed up. This whole thing could have been a commercial for a competitor's cell phone. Bad reception is *so* not a good thing."

Mitchie and Caitlyn were hugging Lola and screeching when Peggy came running up to them. "These all sound like happy sounds," she said, smiling. She looked over at Lola.

"Totally happy sounds!" Lola said, flashing Peggy a huge grin. "I'm sorry that I left you in the middle of the mystery, Peggy. Did you do okay with the clue?"

"Yes," Peggy said, "I totally got it! We're still in the game, partner. Next stop is the B-Note."

"Hey, that's where we're headed," Mitchie said, glad that they could all go together. She was all for winning, but some things—like her friends' happiness—were more important.

Lola smiled, and there was a glint in her eye. "Well, then, you better get moving, because Peggy and I are going to beat you there!" She took off running, her friends hot on her heels.

The good news had inspired the girls, and they all happily raced off to the canteen. But they stopped short when they got to the door and found Tess, Ella, and Lorraine standing outside.

"Don't bother," Tess said. "There is no B-Note clue." She shifted her weight and crossed her arms in front of her chest. "Don't waste your time."

Mitchie eyed Tess. She didn't believe her for one second. And she didn't want to waste any more time talking to her. She moved past her. "Come on, Tess," she said. "We're not going to fall for that move. It's perfectly clear what you are trying to do."

"That is pretty low," Peggy added as she walked past Tess.

Tess pouted her lips and walked off with her entourage. "Whatever," she said. "I tried to be nice."

When the four girls walked inside the B-Note, they were surprised to find Connie sitting at a table lined with cookies shaped like musical notes. "Hey, girls," she called out. "How about some snacks? Freshly baked butter cookies!"

The four girls looked at each other and then back at Connie.

"Wow," Peggy said. "You mean to tell me that Tess was actually telling the truth? I seriously don't believe it."

Caitlyn shook her head. "I was so sure that the B-Note was the right answer. You mean this was a fake-out clue?"

Connie smiled and held up a tray of cookies. "Well, yes, but at least you get a cookie for stopping by."

"Thanks," Lola said as she grabbed one. "Sorry we can't stay, though!"

On their way out the door, the girls bumped into Shane and Brown, who were just walking in.

"How's it going?" Shane asked, smirking. "Visiting B-Note, huh?"

"Ah, I love this game!" Brown said, pleased with himself. "All the hard work really pays off."

"You are all just cruel," Caitlyn said to Brown, even though she had to admit the course—and the B-Note treats—had hit the spot.

Shane laughed. "Oh, come on," he said innocently. "At least this year's fake-out clue had a snack!"

"Gee, thanks," Peggy said as she passed him.

"Chin up, ladies," Brown said encouragingly.

The four girls went back outside and sat down on the grass. They took out the sheet music, and together they once again tried to decipher the clue.

"Yum, these cookies are good," Lola said, taking a bite. Peggy shot her a disbelieving look. "I know, we've got to concentrate," Lola said, shrugging. "But I'm just saying, they *are* good cookies!"

Caitlyn spread the music out on the ground. "If it's not the B-Note, what other clues can we find in the music?"

"There are no words in the clue," Mitchie said, thinking out loud. "So, we can't think about lyrics."

Peggy knelt down closer to the paper. "Wait! We have the same one! This must be leading us to the final clue! So there has to be something we're missing. How about . . . ?" She looked up and smiled at her friends. She had the answer! How could she not have seen it before?

"That's it!" Lola said, as if she were reading Peggy's mind. She bent down and pointed to the upper left-hand corner. "It's not the note—it's the tempo! It says here, *presto*!"

"The rehearsal cabin up on the hill!" Mitchie and Caitlyn said at the same time. While it didn't have an official name, Brown taught one of his classes there.

"I think you've got something," Caitlyn said, her eyes wide.

"But that's clear across camp," Peggy added.

"I think it will be worth the trek," Lola said.

Lola's confidence won over the others, and in a united front, the four of them raced up the hill. When they reached the small rehearsal cabin, they were exhausted and winded. And to make matters worse, when all four arrived, they found Tess, Ella, and Lorraine already there.

"Nice to see you all," Tess said in a voice heavy with sarcasm. "Too bad you didn't listen to me before. I could have saved you the sprint. But now you'll never catch up with us." She waved her orange clue in front of their faces and headed out the door. "See you from the winner's circle!" she said as she strolled off, her entourage close behind as always.

"No way," Lola muttered. "If Tess wins this competition, I'm going to be so mad!"

Caitlyn put her hand out the way a traffic cop would. "Hold on," she said. "Tess hasn't won anything yet. We just need to keep focused and stay on our game."

They each took their color clue and went off to a different part of the cabin to figure out where they were supposed to go next. This time there were actual CDs in their CD cases, not just sheet music. There was also a small slip of paper.

"The final clue!" Caitlyn exclaimed.

"Us, too!" Lola said, holding up the silver CD.

Mitchie looked confused. "The only CD player is at the theater. So, we have to go all the way back to the center of camp and listen?"

Caitlyn nodded her head. "Yup," she said.

"And we better hurry because the last clue is always the hardest one."

"Man, I should have worn my running shoes," Mitchie said, looking down at her flip-flops. "No one explained to me that this was a track-and-field event!"

Her friends laughed as they all jogged back down the hill toward the theater, where they could listen to the final clue . . . and maybe, just maybe, win the prize.

CHAPTER TWELVE

Mitchie and her friends weren't the only ones close to finishing. When they arrived, the theater was filled with teams listening on headphones to their CD clues. It was a little tense. How much time did they really have to figure out this musical mystery?

One of the counselors standing at the door greeted Mitchie and Caitlyn and handed them their earphones and a CD player. She set them up in a row of seats away from the other teams. "There's a strict no-speaking rule while you are in the theater," the counselor told them. "This is a listening library for the afternoon, so please refrain from talking." Then she smiled. "Good luck!"

Mitchie saw Andy and Colby huddled together a few rows ahead. They looked very determined as they sat trying to decipher where their final destination on the mystery hunt might be. Colby looked up and gave Mitchie and Caitlyn a small wave, but Andy didn't even raise his head. Winning was definitely on everyone's mind.

Tess and her crew, on the other hand, were nowhere to be seen. Mitchie knew that those girls could still come in first.

Looking down at her watch, Mitchie realized that time was speeding by.

As Caitlyn placed her earphones on her head, she looked over at Peggy and Lola across the aisle. *Good luck,* she mouthed.

Peggy and Lola both smiled. *You, too!* they both mouthed back, careful not to break the no-talking rule.

Nodding that she was ready, Caitlyn slipped on her headset, and Mitchie pressed PLAY. "Remember," she whispered, "the clue says that it's a well-loved spot in camp." She held up the slip of paper that they had found in the CD case and pointed to the message.

"That could be a hundred places!" Mitchie whispered back, trying not to panic. They were so close to winning!

"Ready?" Caitlyn asked.

"Yes," Mitchie replied. She reached over and took the song list out of the case and looked at the three songs listed. "None of these seem very nature-oriented," she commented. "How are we going to hear any lyrics that lead us to a place on the campgrounds?"

"Shhh," Caitlyn said, holding up her finger to her lips. She looked around the theater. She didn't want to get called out for talking.

The counselor at the front door was showing a new team to its spot, and everyone else had earphones on. "Let's listen to the three songs," she said very quietly to Mitchie.

They sat back in their seats and played the music. They were careful to pay attention to all the words, trying not to miss any subtle clues.

The first song was a Connect Three ballad that had been a top-ten hit earlier in the year. The next song was by Faye Hart, which made Mitchie roll her eyes. She was hardly the pop star's biggest fan. Faye's songs all sounded the same. She had tried to buy one of Mitchie's when she had come up to visit Shane for his Connect Three platinum party; Mitchie had learned a good lesson about the music business—and herself. Her songs were definitely not for sale! The one on the CD was like all of Faye's songs; it had a pulsing beat that gave Mitchie a headache. There were no clues to lead them to any place on the campgrounds. . . .

As the next song started, Mitchie looked over at Caitlyn hopefully. Maybe this final one would hold the clue?

It was quiet in the theater, with just a few hushed whispers. Then the music started to play through their headphones. It was Margaret Dupree! Peggy was singing the song that had one won her first place at Final Jam. Even though Mitchie and Caitlyn were intent on listening for their clue, they couldn't help but be delighted that Dee had included Peggy's song.

After the song ended, Caitlyn took her earphones off. "Well, I got nothing," she said quietly, slumping back in her seat. "Did you hear anything that would give us a clue?"

Mitchie shook her head and looked over the list again. Of the three songs, none of them seemed to have any relation to a place at camp. She was about to give up when she heard the beating of a drum . . . and then some guitar strumming. She hit PAUSE and leaned over closer to Caitlyn. She smiled. "There's another song! A hidden track!" She tried to keep her voice to a low whisper, but she was too excited. Mitchie moved down low in her seat and went on to explain. "Shane's so sneaky! Just like he's planning for his new CD, there's a hidden track here, too!" She grinned knowing that the clue to their mystery had to be somewhere in this final track. "What do you think?"

"I think you're brilliant!" Caitlyn said, tugging her earphones back on.

Mitchie leaned forward and put her elbows on her knees, cradling her head. This had to be the clue! The song wasn't familiar to her, but the voice was—it was Shane! He was strumming his guitar and singing softly. This had to be the new song he was talking about the other night at the B-Note, Mitchie thought. As the song hit the chorus, she heard the clue loud and clear. *"Sit with me at the hollowed-out tree, and together we'll rest and be us for a while."*

Looking over at Mitchie, Caitlyn smiled broadly. "Bingo!" she exclaimed.

Mitchie and Caitlyn quickly returned their equipment to the counselor and raced out the door. They didn't even look around, for fear of being delayed. They had to get to the tree before anyone else figured out the clue! But would they be the first ones there?

CHAPTER THIRTEEN

Glancing up from the CD player in her hands, Lola saw Mitchie and Caitlyn race out of the theater. How could they have gotten the clue so fast? she thought. She had been listening to the songs and nothing sounded like a clue to her! She looked over at Peggy, who had a look of sheer determination on her face.

Tapping Peggy on the arm, Lola pointed to

the door as their friends scooted out. If Mitchie and Caitlyn already knew the answer, that meant they would have a solid head start. Lola was afraid that she and Peggy were doomed.

Because they were distracted by their friends leaving, they didn't realize that Peggy's song had ended. Instead of hitting the button to start the loop again, they let the CD play on . . . and then the bonus track began.

With wide eyes, Peggy held Lola's hand. Where did this song come from? It wasn't on the list that came with the CD. Then, all of a sudden it hit her. She totally got the clue. "A hidden track!" she said softly to Lola.

Lola put her finger to her mouth to keep Peggy from speaking too loudly. She didn't want to fill everyone in on their discovery!

As they listened to Shane's new song, they got the message just as quickly as their friends had. After the first verse, their headphones were off, and they, too, were racing for the door.

Before they left, the two girls took stock of who was still left in the room. They couldn't help but smile when they saw Tess, Ella, and Lorraine sitting in the back row of the theater. Tess was making a sour face, and the other girls were pouting. Clearly, they had not discovered the secret track yet.

"Come on," Peggy said, tugging at Lola's hand. "There's no time to waste. We've got to get a move on!"

"Do you think we can catch up?" Lola asked when they got outside. She looked up the hill toward the hollowed-out tree cited in the hidden track.

"Yes!" Peggy exclaimed as she burst forward. "I have no doubt," she added over her shoulder.

Lola had never seen Peggy move so fast! She ran at full speed up the hill. Somehow they'd have to make up time and get to the tree first!

As they came around the corner, they saw Brown, Dee, Shane, and a few other counselors. They all appeared to be looking at something. Peggy squinted her eyes, but she couldn't tell what they were doing. Then she heard them give a cheer, and her heart sank. There was already a winner. . . .

"At least it was Mitchie and Caitlyn," Lola said as she slowed her pace. "They can tell us all about the recording with Connect Three."

"Oh, no, we can't," Mitchie said, coming over. She and Caitlyn had reached the tree—but too late. "We didn't get here first."

Peggy's jaw dropped open. "What? So, who won?" She craned her neck to see who was at the center of the circle ahead.

"Colby and Andy," Caitlyn told them. "They got here right before we did. Just a few seconds, really. Talk about a total bummer!"

"But totally fair," Mitchie said, shaking

her head. "I'm happy for them—they worked hard."

"And they should be *very* happy," Shane said, walking over to join the girls. "They get to perform on a Connect Three CD."

Mitchie gave Shane a playful hit on his arm. "Very sneaky placing the clue in a hidden track! We almost had the prize!"

Shane smiled. "I told you that the hidden tracks are what CD sales are all about now. You've got to keep the audience wanting more."

"Well, now I will definitely be listening to Connect Three's hidden tracks," Mitchie said as they all began, walking toward the two winners. "I bet those will be the best parts of the album." She winked at her friends Colby and Andy.

The winners grinned. "Thanks, Mitchie," Colby said. "It's hard to believe we actually did it."

"Well, believe it," Shane said, smiling. "It's

going to be a lot of fun . . . and hard work. You up for all that?"

Colby and Andy nodded. "Yes!" they shouted at the same time, huge grins on their faces.

Soon more teams started showing up at the hollowed-out tree. Everyone had eventually figured out that there was an additional song on the CD and understood the clue. Finally Tess, Ella, and Lorraine arrived. All three looked annoyed.

"My agent wouldn't like me singing on a hidden track anyway," Tess said as she passed Mitchie and her friends. "He's all about me taking on more starring positions. You know, I am the perfect candidate for a solo career."

Mitchie, Caitlyn, Peggy, and Lola all looked at each other and laughed as Tess strutted by.

"Does she even have an agent?" Mitchie whispered to Caitlyn.

"In her own mind," Caitlyn replied, rolling her eyes.

Exhausted from their busy day, the girls found a shady spot so they could sit down and rest. For snacks, Connie and some of the counselors were handing out ice pops. The cool treat was perfect for the tired—and very hot—campers.

Mitchie massaged her aching calves with her hands. "Man, this mystery hunt was a serious workout. No one told me this would be a musical marathon! My legs are killing me!"

"I don't think I've ever run that much at any camp!" Peggy said, flopping on her back. She let out a huge sigh.

Caitlyn laughed. "Yeah, but it was worth it. This, by far, was the best musical mystery Camp Rock ever had."

"Even if we didn't win," Peggy said, frowning.

"Well, at least I don't have to leave on a

losing note," Lola exclaimed. She slurped her cherry ice pop happily. "As long as I can stay at camp for the whole session, I'm good." She smiled. "I wasn't ready to leave Camp Rock yet."

"Oh, don't talk about leaving," Caitlyn fretted. "I can't stand to think about saying good-bye to this place." Then she looked around at her friends. "And you guys, of course."

Mitchie reached out and gave her friends a big hug. "We've still got lots of music to make," she said, smiling.

"And a few more jams and prizes to win," Caitlyn added. "This summer is far from over!"

The four girls let out a loud cheer. "To Camp Rock!" they cried, raising their ice pops in a colorful salute. "And to more of the best summer ever!"

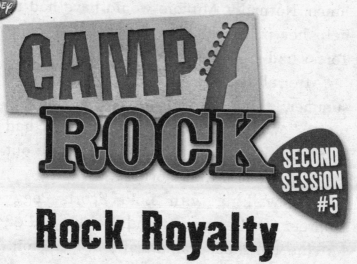

Rock Royalty

By Lucy Ruggles

Based on "Camp Rock," Written by Karin Gist & Regina Hicks and Julie Brown & Paul Brown

The sun was high over Camp Rock, and stomachs were growling. After a full morning of dance practice, voice lessons, and swimming, Mitchie Torres was famished. She

111

couldn't wait to see what her mom, Camp Rock's chef-in-residence, had whipped up for lunch. Normally, Mitchie would have had to help her in the kitchen, but today Connie Torres had given her daughter the day off.

"After all the parties I've had to cater this summer, I think I can handle a little old lunch on my own for once!" Mitchie's mom had assured her, practically pushing Mitchie out the kitchen door that morning.

Now, walking with Lola Scott, Peggy Dupree, and her best friend, Caitlyn Geller, Mitchie clutched dramatically at her stomach. "Who knew hip-hop could take so much out of a girl!" she cried.

"Yeah," agreed Peggy. "That new move Shane's teaching us—the Crush—is killing me. I just can't seem to get it down."

"Speaking of crushes," said Lola, raising a mischievous eyebrow, "I think someone at Camp Rock might have one on Caitlyn."

Caitlyn's mouth fell open. She blushed as

Mitchie, Lola, and Peggy began to giggle. Lola's observation wasn't a surprise. It had become obvious that a certain camper who had come to Camp Rock for Second Session had taken a special interest not just in the music Caitlyn liked to produce on her laptop, but in the producer herself.

Caitlyn immediately sputtered out a protest. "Mac does *not* have a crush on me!"

"I didn't mention Mac." Lola grinned. "You did."

Caitlyn turned a deeper shade of magenta, and the other girls laughed harder.

Mac Wilson was Colby Miller's bunk mate. The two newbies had become friends even though they were wildly different. Colby was a preppy New Englander while Mac was a Southern boy who played guitar, always quick with a smile and a greeting. Mac was one of those people who got along with everyone—especially Caitlyn.

"Well, I think he's cute," Mitchie said,

coming to Caitlyn's aid. "His drawl is adorable."

"What's wrong with meeting someone a little extraspecial at camp?" Peggy shrugged. "It worked for Mitchie."

Now it was Mitchie's turn to turn bright red. It was true that Mitchie and Shane Gray, lead singer of the hot band Connect Three and Camp Rock instructor, had formed a special friendship over the summer. Despite his bad-boy reputation and rock-star attitude upon first arriving at camp, Shane was actually really cool. He and Mitchie just *got* each other. Mitchie had helped Shane get back to his own sound, and he had helped her find her confidence onstage. Still, their friendship was a subject that made Mitchie shy.

Caitlyn laughed and threw her arm around her friend's shoulder. Just as she was about to make a joke, the deafening sound of a propeller drowned her out. The wind whipped around them, blowing Mitchie's long, brown hair in her face. All at once, every camper walking toward the Mess Hall of Fame turned his or her face to the sky. It was a helicopter—and it was heading right for Camp Rock!

More campers spilled out of the B-Note canteen in the mess hall's basement and down the paths from the cabins. They all wanted to see whose chopper was descending on Camp Rock's front lawn. They stood with their mouths hanging open as the huge aircraft touched down on the grass.

A moment later, pop sensation T.J. Tyler stepped out of the helicopter.

The singer shook her long, blond hair out of her face and scanned the growing crowd. T.J. had some exciting news for her daughter Tess, a camper at Camp Rock. She'd decided a surprise visit was in order. T.J. wanted to tell Tess in person.

Besides being an award-winning, multi-platinum recording artist, T.J. Tyler was also the face of Blush Cosmetics. Blush had decided to sponsor a special concert to raise money for after-school music programs. And they wanted their spokesmodel to perform. Knowing how much Tess had enjoyed the music education she'd gotten this summer at Camp Rock, T.J. was more than happy to help. And when Tess heard the *other* news, she would be more than happy to help, too.

"Mom!" Tess cried, breaking through the circle of campers and rushing to her mother as she came down the helicopter stairs.

"Hi, babe," said T.J. as they air kissed each other on both cheeks. "I'm on my way to a photo shoot for Blush, but I just heard from Ginger and wanted to stop by to tell you—"

"Tell me what?!" Tess interrupted, her blue eyes wide. She couldn't begin to imagine what was so important that her mom had interrupted her busy schedule and come all the way to Camp Rock.

T.J. smiled. She knew her daughter got her

impatient streak from her. "Blush is sponsoring School Rocks, a concert to raise money for after-school music programs . . ."

"Oh." Tess's face deflated. Just another fund-raiser that would take up her mom's time.

". . . *and* they want you and me to perform— together." T.J. continued, beaming.

"Me?" Tess repeated, her eyes growing large. A real concert? She would be a house-hold name before the program was over!

Ella Pador and Lorraine Burgess, Tess's entourage and best friends, had rushed to her side when they saw the helicopter. Now they started jumping up and down, clapping.

"You're gonna be famous!" Ella squealed.

"O.M.G.," gushed Lorraine. "This is so awesome!"

"So, I'll take that as a yes?" T.J. grinned.

Tess nodded her head enthusiastically. "Yes!" she screamed. Then composing her-self, she said casually, "I'll do it," as if she was agreeing to take out the trash, not sing in a major concert.

"Wonderful," said a happy T.J. "I'll let Ginger know. Gotta jet, babe. Annie's waiting at the photo studio, and she *hates* when the talent's late. I'll call you about the details later."

T.J. and Tess double-air-kissed again, and just as quickly as she had appeared, T.J. was gone.

The must-have book for any fan of *High School Musical*!

SECRET PASSWORD FOR AN EXCLUSIVE WEB PAGE AND **HIGH SCHOOL MUSICAL 3: SENIOR YEAR** DOWNLOADS INSIDE!

With lots of removable extras!

Disney PRESS   **AVAILABLE WHEREVER BOOKS ARE SOLD**